For Ryan, Christie, and Ramona
—G.P.

Text copyright © 2018 by Cirocco Dunlap
Cover art and interior illustrations copyright © 2018 by Greg Pizzoli
All rights reserved. Published in the United States by Dragonfly Books, an imprint of Random House Children's Books,
a division of Penguin Random House LLC, New York. Originally published in hardcover in the United States by
Random House Children's Books, a division of Penguin Random House LLC, New York, in 2018.

Dragonfly Books and colophon are registered trademarks of Penguin Random House LLC.

Visit us on the Web! rhcbooks.com
Educators and librarians, for a variety of teaching tools, visit us at RHTeachersLibrarians.com

Library of Congress Cataloging-in-Publication Data is available upon request.
ISBN 978-0-593-17568-2 (pbk.)

Book design by Martha Rago
MANUFACTURED IN CHINA
10 9 8 7 6 5 4 3 2 1
First Dragonfly Books Edition

Cirocco Dunlap

CRUNCH
The Shy Dinosaur

PICTURES BY
Greg Pizzoli

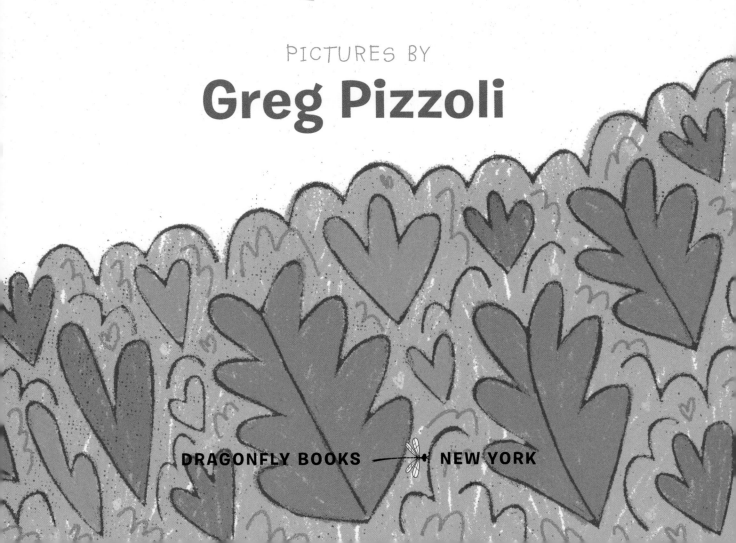

DRAGONFLY BOOKS ⟶ NEW YORK

This is Crunch.

Crunch is shy, so you'll have to be the first to say hello.

Go on, say **hello.**

Oh my, you've said it too loudly.
Crunch seems to have run off.

Do you see him anywhere?

He likes the "Happy Birthday" song.
Do you know that song?

If you sing it, maybe he'll
come out.

It worked—he's out!

He loves birthdays because
someone has one every day.

He loves days in general.
He's very positive.

Try to say hello again!

**You can try it quietly
so you don't scare him.**

That was TOO QUIET.

He's gotten
UNCOMFORTABLY CLOSE
to you.

Try it one more time,
in a nice
medium-sounding
voice.

Bold, yet gentle.

Perfect.

You can tell he liked that because he's an appropriate distance from you, and also because he put on his most fun hat and is dancing.

Now you can tell him your name!

Say it clearly so he can paint it on that big rock. He loves painting names.

There's your name, perfectly painted!

You can't see it because it's behind a big pile of leaves.

Say Thank you, Crunch!

Your voice startled him.

Maybe now would be a good time
to be very quiet, and very still,
and see if he climbs back down.

Good job being so quiet
and still.

**Sometimes it's important to let shy
dinosaurs come to you at their own pace.**

Crunch is tired from all the climbing and painting and socializing.

You can remind him he should go
to sleep by saying **Good night,
Crunch.**

He must have thought you said Good light, Crunch.

Say **Good night, Crunch,** one more time, in a calm and soothing voice.

Maybe you can lie down when you say it, to show him how nice sleep is.

You did it!
He passed out immediately.

We should probably let him sleep.

If you wouldn't mind, please
close this book VERY gently.